To Mum and Dad for all the stories
and to Lou, for always being there for me.

Imprint
A part of Macmillan Publishing Group, LLC
175 Fifth Avenue, New York, NY 10010

About This Book
Artist's medium is acrylic, gouache and digital media.
The text was set in Fanwood, and the display type is KG All of Me.
FERGAL AND THE BAD TEMPER. Copyright © 2017, 2019 by Robert Starling.
All rights reserved. Printed and bound by Toppan Leefung, China.
Library of Congress Cataloging-in-Publication Data is available.
ISBN 978-1-250-19862-4 (hardcover)

Our books may be purchased in bulk for promotional, educational, or business use.
Please contact your local bookseller or the Macmillan Corporate and
Premium Sales Department at (800) 221-7945 ext. 5442 or by e-mail
at MacmillanSpecialMarkets@macmillan.com.
Imprint logo designed by Amanda Spielman
Originally published in the United Kingdom by
Andersen Press, Ltd. in 2017.
First US edition, 2019
1 3 5 7 9 10 8 6 4 2
mackids.com

Fergal's a nice little dragon,
but if you pilfer this book
he could get very, very ANGRY!

ROBERT STARLING

FERGAL
AND THE
BAD TEMPER

NEW YORK

This is Fergal.
What a nice dragon!

He's a friendly little fellow.

But when someone
tells him what to do,
Fergal gets very . . .

very . . .

ANGRY.

Like when his dad said,
"Fergal, come down for your dinner!"

But Fergal wanted to keep playing.

And then he said
Fergal had to eat all
his vegetables if he
wanted dessert.

Fergal felt fiery.

"It's **not**
FAIR!"

So Fergal didn't get any dessert,
and he didn't get any dinner, either.

Fergal got in a pickle
on the soccer field.

YOU'RE GOALKEEPER!

"It's **not** FAIR!" said Fergal.

"I don't want to be the . . ."

KAWUMFFF!

"...goalkeeper."

His fiery temper got Fergal into trouble all over town.

Wherever he went, Fergal just couldn't keep his cool.

Finally his friends had had enough.

"Everyone's ignoring
me, Mom,"
said Fergal.

"It's **not**
FAIR!"

"Well Fergal, dinner is in the trash, Bear's pastries are burned
and no one can play soccer, and that's not fair."

"We all get fiery," sighed Mom, "but we find a way
to cool down. My trick is to count to ten."

The next day,
Fergal felt
fiery again.

"That's **not** . . ."

But then he remembered his mom's trick . . .

"**ONE!
TWO!**
THREE. Four.
Five . . ."

. . . and he didn't feel so fiery.

It had worked!

Fergal noticed lots of animals had their own way to cool down.

When Crow felt
fiery, he told his
friends about it.

When Fox felt fiery,

he watched the sunset.

Wolf always found a nice
quiet spot and made a
BIG NOISE!

a WOOOOOOOOOOOOOO

Cat lay back and had a really good stretch.

And then there was Hare: whizzing about
stopped her feeling fiery in the first place.

Now Fergal had lots of ways to
cool down, and when he didn't waste
his fire on being angry . . .

. . . he found there were much more interesting things to do with it.